The

Deed

of

Gift

To Tom
From Tim Murphy
for auld lange syne

The
Deed
of
Gift

Timothy Murphy

STORY LINE PRESS

1998

Published by Story Line Press, Inc.
Three Oaks Farm
PO Box 1108
Ashland OR 97520-0052

This publication was made possible thanks in part to the
generous support of the Nicholas Roerich Museum, and our
individual contributors.

Book design by Paul Joseph Pope

Library of Congress Cataloging-in-Publication Data

Murphy, Timothy, 1951-
      The deed of gift : poems / Timothy Murphy.
         p. cm
      ISBN 1-885266-62-6
      1. Farm life—Poetry. 2. Homosexuality—Poetry. 3. Title.
I. Title.
PS3563.U7619D44 1998
811'.54—dc21   98-14326
                                              CIP

for my collaborator

Alan Sullivan

If you curse me for my verse
catch a cricket by the wing
and shout at it for chirping.

—Archilochus

Acknowledgements

Thanks to the editors of the following publications:
*The Hudson Review, The New Criterion, Hellas,
The Epigrammatist, Sparrow, Light, The Dark Horse,
The Formalist, Canadian Alpine Journal, Mockingbird,
Christopher Street, Prop, Chronicles, Janus, Carolina
Quarterly, The Edge City Review*

Many of these poems have also appeared in two
chapbooks:
Bedrock, The Aralia Press, 1998
The Ant Lion, Robert L. Barth, 1996

Contents

III. The Gift of Hera

IV. Father of the Man

V. Early Poems

Preface

It has been my pleasure to correspond with Timothy Murphy for many years, and to see him develop his gifts in the direction of this book, which rewards his patience and will reward anyone who reads it. His is a truly distinctive talent. Though he has, in fact, done vigorous, supple work in our basic pentameter measure—in "The Failure," for example, or in the wittily-turned early poem "Waiting for Octavian"—one thing that sets him apart is that he has latterly inclined toward talking in short meters. He acknowledges that inclination, all too modestly, in his "Letter to A. D. Hope." A reader will find, on entering the first section of the book, that the poems are slender and on the whole brief; and he will also find them to be resourcefully rhymed. A further finding, which the reader will make at once, is that despite the technical challenges which Murphy sets himself and meets, the voice of the poem is not that of a daredevil formalist or nifty technician, rather it is the voice of a Dakota farmer who knows everything about outrageous extremes of weather, crop failure, and the many adversities which can lead to falling-down barns and ghost towns. That voice knows what things are and how they go, and even in a poem of virtuoso rhyme like "Harvest of Sorrows" the music is subordinate to the facts given, and the feelings that go with the facts. If I tried to say what it means for these poems to be so songlike, I think I would say that I hear in their music the jauntiness of a survivor, and the high morale of a man who has a purchase on reality, however bleak.

Other themes occupy the other sections of *The Deed of Gift*, and are explored in spare poems which, at their best, are worthy of the Frost of "Beech" and "Dust of Snow" and "Away!" I shall say no more here except to

assure the reader that the author of "The Peg-leg Pig,"
"Poem for Noam," "The Cave," "The Hatch," and "Jas-
per Lake" has many good things to show him.

> Richard Wilbur
> Key West
> 21 February 1997

The
Deed
of
Gift

I.

Farming
All
Night

Twice Cursed

Bristling with fallen trees
and choked with broken ice
the river threatens the house.
I'll wind up planting rice
if the spring rains don't cease.
What ancestral curse
prompts me to farm and worse,
convert my woes to verse?

The Expulsion

Six weeks of drought,
the corn undone
and wheat burned out
by the brazen sun—

over that land
an angel stands
with an iron brand
singeing his hands.

Eighty-eight at Midnight

A black calf bleats
at shrivelled teats.
Incessant heat
withers the wheat
and wilts the silking corn.
Too few, too late
the spotty showers
mock my stunted flowers.
Too late I shrink from debt.
Like a spitted calf I turn
over a bed of coals
while the pastures burn.

The Godless Sky

Airborne, I view the flood.
  Flattened wheat
  blackens in the heat
or smothers under mud.

In the Piper's path I spot
  the farmstead
  on the home spread
my father's father bought.

An uncle stauncher than I
  bears the cross
  of another loss
under the godless sky.

The Oats of Wrath

"You want cash in a trust?"
the farmer scolds his son.
Dark as drifted dust
after the seed has blown,
stark as hardpan crust
cracking under the sun,
he bellows as he must:
"Your grandfather went bust.
I saved the goddam farm!"
Hair laid flat by the gust,
a boy waits out the storm.

Hoggerel

How many pigs
can dance on a pin?
the banker oinks
with a swinish grin.

Our boars are lean;
our sows are silk,
ready to milk
and quick to wean.

Meal and corn
sell for a song,
and bellies
jump over the moon.

Handsome Dan

Like a horny boar
sniffing a sow,
he was eager to lend
on hardscrabble ground.

Now the hapless man
who shook the hand
of handsome Dan
loses his family's land.

Like a squealing sow
on the slaughterhouse floor
he forfeits his life
to the banker's knife.

The Peg-leg Pig

A farmer's daughter keeps a hog
who sports a wooden leg.
"Tell me about that peg-leg pig,"
travelling salesmen beg.

"He saved me from a rabid skunk.
He stomped it with his peg."
Suspiciously a seed man squints:
"How did he lose the leg?"

"He found me when a whiteout hit
and led me through the snow."
"You called the vet to amputate?
A case of frostbite?" *"No.*

"He pulled me from a flaming barn
before the rafters fell."
"Enough to put me off my corn.
It must have hurt like hell."

"Who said my peg-leg pig was lamed?
He never got a scratch."
"That leg is missing all the same.
Sister, what's the catch?

"Was it chomped on by a bigger pig
or torn off by a plough,
squashed beneath a threshing rig
or trampled by a cow?

"Was the porker born to walk on wood
or crippled in his prime?"
"Mister, you eat a pig this good
one leg at a time."

Shep's Last Stand

for Rich Bell

A flyblown German shepherd
lay in the buckshot-peppered
finishing barn
the day we bought the farm.

Brave dog,
he fought to the last hog
as the Norway rats
swarmed over the slats.

Kelly's Lament

for Kelly Miller

I fear for my spring wheat.
Will it grow hard and tall
  or head out small?
Will it succumb to heat,
  drought and dust
  or rot and rust?
Will it be flooded out
or flattened by the hail?
  I am beset
  by doubt and debt.
Surely the wheat will fail.

Harvest of Sorrows

When swift brown swallows
return to their burrows
and diamond willows
leaf in the hollows,
when barrows wallow
and brood sows farrow,
we sow the black furrows
behind our green harrows.

When willows yellow
in the windy hollows,
we butcher the barrows
and fallow the prairies.
The silo swallows
a harvest of sorrows;
the ploughshare buries
a farmer's worries.

Now harried sparrows
forage in furrows.
Lashing the willows,
the north wind bellows
while farmers borrow
on unborn barrows.
Tomorrow, tomorrow
the sows will farrow.

Spring Song

Oh the grouse are loudly drumming
and raucous geese are crying.
Summertime is coming,
flocks of ducks are flying,
Lovesick lads are sighing
and bumblebees are humming.

Oh the hummingbird is sucking
nectar from a lily
and the yearling colt is bucking
an unwilling filly.
Squirrels are scolding shrilly
and sparrows wildly fucking.

Chapter Seven

Chicken neck
on a chopping block,
I sow my crops
and the hatchet drops.

Gray and cold
as a day in court,
I'm too soon old,
too late smart.

Failures of Promise

A flock of crows
found a road-killed ewe
frozen in the snow.
A drowsy bear
dragged a leg-shot deer
to its deadfall lair.
The lamb in the ewe
and the fawn in the doe
were devoured unborn,
and November snows
buried the standing corn.

Farming All Night

I dreamed of a lush stand of hard spring wheat
    and bumper barley yields
      ripening in my fields,
sunflowers blooming in the summer heat—

then came the black squalls with swathes of hail,
    lodged and battered grain,
      ruinous harvest rain
and flooded barley rotting in the swale.

Next Year, Locusts

Plough the stubble. Set the drawbar deep.
    Let the north winds blow,
      smothering the fields in snow.
Farmers and the depleted soil must sleep

before the thistle thrusts a thorny shoot
    from its bristling corm,
      hatching locusts swarm
and the first cutworm chews a tender root.

A Farmer's Prayer

Spirit of the wheat
brush every beard
turning green flaxen
with a wave of your wand.
The wind is your oven,
the hills your loaves.
Dry husks rustle,
flag leaves furl,
heads curl earthward
as kernels harden.
Your garden is golden,
your larder laden.
Feed a hungry world.

Babushka

Her hair tied in a knot,
she hoes her garden plot:

"Six feet by three
is land enough for me."

The Failure

Tractor and combine axle-deep in muck,
seedcorn and soybeans frozen in the field,
the home farm pledged against a bumper yield,
he has run out of money, time and luck.

What would his frugal Swedish forebears think
to see their hard-won holdings on the block?
There is no solace for a laughing-stock
in woman's arms, religion or strong drink.

Any day now the banker will foreclose,
summon the sheriff and the auctioneers.
What will he tell his sons in twenty years?
He cannot wholly blame the early snows.

Betting the Ranch

He could have sold his pregnant cows last fall.
    A hedger ought to weigh
    the cost of air-dropped hay
before a blizzard and a margin call.

Center Pivots

Fields of canola
on the plains of Montana:
slices of banana
in a bowl of granola.

Buffalo Commons

In Antler, Reeder,
Ryder and Streeter,
stray dogs bristle
when strangers pass.

In Brocket, Braddock,
Maddock and Wheelock
dry winds whistle
through broken glass.

The steeples are toppled
and the land unpeopled,
reclaimed by thistle
and buffalo grass.

II.

Je
Me
Souviens

The Forsaken Isle

Homing flocks
of guillemots
and lesser auks
nest on the rocks.

Seals whelp
on windrowed kelp,
and kittiwakes
shriek at the sheep.

Lichens blacken
broken headstones
forgotten
in the bracken.

Castles crumble,
and huddled
hovels tumble
into rubble.

Songs of the North

I. The Weaver

Her loom is bone
and her comb, baleen.
The yarn is wool
from an arctic ox
spun with the down
of eider ducks.
She summons whales,
spotted seals
and narwhals
to a bloodstained beach.
She conjures hunters
blown astray
on the windy reach
of Baffin Bay.
Tidal shallows,
glacial gravel,
stunted willows
and ptarmigan,
she weaves, unravels
and weaves again.

II. The Barrens

The snowy owl
swoops on a vole.
White wolves howl
on a moonlit hill.
But no hunter
waits for the herd
or hears the thunder
of hooves at the ford.
A pox from the South
has emptied the North.

III. Three Foxes

The red fox sleeps in the woods
under a roof of roots.
The long-eared desert fox
dens in the weathered rocks.
But when the blizzards wail
the Arctic fox curls its tail
over its frosty nose
and sleeps in the snows.

IV. Grønland

The last ship sails;
the barley fails.
Only the bones
of the Danes remain.
Marmots peer
from the felsenmeer,
and the wise ravens
at Jakobshavn
breed in the lemming years.

V. Man of the North

I am a wall of rock,
a raucous rookery
where thieving skuas flock.
I am a sunlit sea
where murres and puffins splash
into the tinkling brash.
I am the slaughtered whales,
walruses and seals,
the storm-shredded sails
and bleached, skeletal keels
of whalers run aground
with all hands drowned.

Je Me Souviens

The Laurentian Bar
at Chateau Frontenac,
a Cuban cigar
and a Grand Armagnac
transported me back
with Montcalm and his men
to the siege of Quebec.
Je me souviens.

Martinique

*C'est un jour
de malheur.
Les bateaux,
les oiseaux
s'enfuillent
de la plage;
les nuages
et les vagues
sont troubles.
Dans mon coeur
une lordeure
et une langue
étrangére.*

Montego Boy

His limbs were lean as mangrove roots
    and his skin nutmeg brown.
I followed him past the charter boats
    as the swollen sun went down.

When he cast me adrift at midnight,
    wafting home to his island girls,
his fingernails in the wan moonlight
    shone like a strand of pearls.

Somewhere the swell thumps on a beach
    and a boy wanders the sand
while I stand watch on a red-eyed reach
    between the reefs and land.

Bitter End

A moonlit league to larboard
curls a reef where breakers pound,
but we lie snugly harbored
in Virgin Gorda Sound.

Battening down my mainsail,
I picture the Fastnet fleet
beating into a force ten gale
no skipper meant to meet.

The keepers of the Fastnet Light
tended their spinning lens,
wondering who would sleep that night
with good Sir Patrick Spens.

On the shallows of Labadie Bank
the cresting billows burst.
Many a vessel broached and sank,
never to finish first.

Long, long will the widows be
weeping upon the strand
for fifteen sailors put to sea
not at a king's command

but driven by some principle
unfathomed as the waves
which pluck men from a capsized hull
and suck them to their graves.

Through the Looking Mask

The queen angelfish
and princess parrotfish
review the sergeant majors
and red-coated soldiers.

A shy hamlet
flees a fairy basslet
while foureye butterflies
flutter round anemones.

Tidal currents ruffle
corky finger corals.
A sorrel seahorse
leaps a purple seafan.

I would bridle that sorrel,
swing into the saddle
and battle a moray
for its coral castle.

Ambergris Cay, Belize

Bad Medicine

Under a rising gibbous moon
Bad Medicine lies still.
The lamentations of a loon
echo from hill to hill.
Susurrous pines and birches
have hushed to hear the loon,
and not a cloud besmirches
the luster of the moon.

The lake shimmers with ringlets
wherever walleyes leap.
Beyond its rocky inlet
serried spruces sleep,
and a twisted silver ribbon
spills from the hills above.
I would build my love a cabin
in that resin-scented grove.

When moose browse in the meadows
and bats flit overhead,
when horned owls haunt the shadows
and chipmunks quake with dread,
when the Great Bear is quailing
at the coming of the moon,
we would listen to the wailing
of the lovelorn loon.

Jasper Lake

Perched on a granite peak
where golden eagles shriek
my love and I peer down
watching the Rockies drown—
crag and evergreen
sunk in aquamarine.
Over the lake last night
speckled trout took flight,
leaping the mirrored moon.
Now in the warmth of noon
gullied glaciers groan,
pouring silt and stone
into the seething streams.
Brief! Brief! a marmot screams,
diving under the scree
as its mountain heads for the sea.

Lonesome Peak

I bed down by a man
whose face like mine is lined
by sunshine and time.
Like mine his back is strained,
his pack travel-stained.
Snowmelt from the Yellowstone
courses through his veins.

Return to the Beartooth

Each year our packs grow heavier
and glacial torrents deeper.
Cutthroat trout are savvier
and switchbacks steeper.
We have outgrown our ardor.
Nights are colder,
groundbeds harder,
and the lovers on the shoulder
of the mountain older.

The Quarrel

Climbing in sullen silence past treeline
where blasted spruces drunkenly incline,
we stumble on two racks of caribou.
Clasped in a deadlock neither bull could break
they bleach beside a frigid Yukon lake—
amateurs who never locked horns with you.

Destruction Bay, Yukon

After Thunder

Storm, thunder no more.
Arroyos, dowse your roar.
Rubber rabbitbush,
antelope bitterbrush
Mormon tea, saxifrage
and Great Basin sage,
sweeten the sorrel plain.
No passion without pain
nor blossoms without rain.

Canyon de Chelly

Love tarries another year
though passions ebb and flow
like freshets fed by snow

or dart like fleeting deer
in ochre petroglyphs
weathering on the cliffs.

Bedrock

Though I endure the shore
　　Moorish villas
　　bougainvilleas
surely I love you more

by waterfalls than fountains
　　for our friendship
　　came of hardship
wandering the mountains.

III.

The
Gift
of
Hera

Two Songs for Richard Wilbur

I. Lament for the Makers

Auden lost in clerihews
Crane vanished on a cruise
Thomas gone at thirty-nine.
Whiskey and wine.

Berryman a suicide
Kees swallowed by the tide
Roethke dragged from his pool.
Laudanum and demerol.

Do you owe longevity
to your art's felicity
or tolerance of pain
acquired grain by grain?
Only you remain.

II. The Last Believer

When like a clipper ship
chafing to leave its slip
you reach beyond our world
when your mast sets in the West
with all sails unfurled
I'll pipe you to your rest
praising a measured voice
that teaches unbelievers to rejoice.

Letter to A.D. Hope

Sir, pardon this unheralded address
from America's Outback. I confess
you daunt me with your storm-wracked *Isle Of Aves*
where shipwrecked sailors wager with the waves
while two striplings couple beneath a spar
by the sage sufferance of your scholar-tar
who grants my love and me the tolerance
our hidebound fathers have denied their sons.

Like yours my lines and themes were once writ large.
Alas! my lame pentameters lacked charge.
Heroic couplets? I abandoned hope,
dazzled by one man's art, another's scope.
Dimeter and trimeter I devise
more skillfully, though slant rhyme is my vice.
Forewarned (the very word is like a curse)
please weigh these gleanings from a farmer's verse.

Mine is a rustic art unlike your own:
no high flown musings on a graven bone
nor gowns cast off for trysts with the unknown,
no successors driven to the despair
suffered daily by your unworthy heir.
Though the estate of poetry seems grim,
young men must hope when prospects look most dim.
I am your servant and disciple—

Tim.

To His Dead Master

You gave me a stone
wrapped in a rag,
a jug, a song
and a tattered coat.
I buried the stone,
drained the jug
and burned the coat.
But I sang the song.
Like a barbed hook
it stuck in my throat.

March 17, 1990

Paddler and Dabbler

You were the white swan
alighting on my pond.
I was the puddle duck
you startled into flight
by trumpeting your song.

The Irish Problem

I.

He sings a verse
without a drink
to loosen his tongue.
A flagon of beer
whispers a curse
in his Irish ear.
Slaked by the song
his thirst is gone
and he is drunk.

II.

Thistles invade our grains;
flowers inured to force
lower their heads and kneel
to the case-hardened steel
drawn by a plodding horse.
Only the plough complains.

The Deed of Gift

When Frost quavered for Kennedy
    I didn't understand
how tenuous is our tenancy
    in this untitled land.

How should we mourn a President
    whom Hollywood embraced,
an aristocratic miscreant
    with literary taste?

Under a graveyard's mossy wall
    Frost rests his snowy head.
"This death impoverishes us all,"
    our short-lived leader said.

Poem for Noam

What grammars we contrive:
the infinitive *to give*
is the active of *have*
whose passive voice is *save.*
The irregular *forgive*
is the perfect tense of *love*
whose antonym is *leave,*
while *grief* is the possessive
of either *life* or *love.*

Deconstruction

Rummaging in rubble
critics are scribbling
like fieldmice nibbling
in a farmer's stubble.

June Bugs

June bugs careen
night after night
against my screen.

In their desire
for warmth and light
they too expire.

The Ant Lion

I bake in a crater,
a sandy amphitheater
whose pitch steepens
as my thirst worsens
and the pit deepens.
When ants and beetles
tumble down my funnel,
I drain them like bottles
whose liquor only quickens
my larval urge to fly,
copulate and die.

Memo to Theognis

No man is happy
unless he loves
smooth-hooved horses,
hunting dogs and boys.

Happy with boys,
horses and dogs?
No man enjoys
a boy's esteem for long.
Horses go to the dogs,
and dogs die young.

Infernal Sonet

Which would provoke more joy,
to ravish you with Donne's
Holy Sonets or poke your buns?
    Cheeky boy
sleeker than any lumpish lass,
stop squirming and hear me read.
Your mind has greater need
of stuffing than your ass.

Sinfonietta

I. An Oak in Amherst

Her attic—like a bark—
floats by the grounded oak
which bears a twisting mark—
doubtless a lightning stroke.

II. Da Trowie Burn

My kinsman, Aly Bain,
comforts a troubled mind
by fiddling for the slain
my forebears left behind.

III. The Hatch

Over the sodden ditches
midges and mayflies swarm,
harbingers of riches
and offspring of the storm.

IV. A Love of Kind

Scribblers to be rid of,
poets I shall discard
when I dispense with love:
Anacreon, Ronsard.

The Cave

Between sleeping and waking
lies a passage I have sought,
a secret passage snaking
through the labyrinth of thought.
But day is always breaking
and the mind bent on waking,
and my consciousness is caught
in a cave of its own making.

Yggdrasil

I am the least leaf
on the tiniest twig
of an unseen tree
inconceivably
bigger than me.

Black Tuesday

A time to cut losses:
in moments of crisis
human sacrifices
are hammered to crosses.
Nothing less suffices.

Ash Wednesday

Dust to dust says the priest,
but Grief is unimpressed:
*How brief was the feast
at your mother's breast.*

The Platonist

An ex-priest in the park—
with downcast eyes he sees
the trees beneath the trees
drink deeply in the dark.

Requiem

To mourn a fallen friend
claimed by untimely death,
I beg the winds to send
the gift of living breath.
Fill my unworthy lungs;
raise my unwilling head.
Why are we born with tongues
if not to praise the dead?

Carpe Diem

Ask not, Leuconoe—we cannot know—
what waits for you or me before we go.
Cast no Chaldean horoscopes, my love,
but take whatever comes. The will of Jove
may grant us more winters or just this one
which now dashes the gray Tyrrhenean
to weariness against our Tuscan cliff.
Wiser to pour the wine: our life is brief
and while we speak the moment flits away.
Place no faith in the future. Seize the day.

Horace, Odes 1:11

Leonardo

Whether for love of flight or liberty,
he bought caged birds only to set them free.

Fame

Mockery is bitter
as arthritis to a knitter.
Flattery is sweeter
than a liter of cognac
to a dypsomaniac.
Knit for eternity.
Drink in anonymity.

Chuang Tzu Takes a Nap

When I was a wizened poet
dozing at my desk
I dreamed I was a cygnet
peeping in its nest.

When I was a tundra swan
migrating by the moon
I dreamed I was a poet
imagining a swan.

Scaling Parnassus

"And who remembers them?"
—A. L. Rowse

Dragonflies whose wings
flutter in sultry air
between the olive trees
crisscross a limestone stair
climbed by Simonides
and some forgotten kings.

La Langue Des Troubadours

"Benvengut," says a sign
on Diocletian's wall.
Like the paté and wine
the tongue is Provençal.
Under the sycamores
where a Roman fountain brims,
I read the troubadours—
thanks to John Frederick Nims—
and young Arnaut Daniel
stung by a woman's scorn
weeps at this limestone well
while Bernard de Ventadorn
laments *"Que planh e plor"*
in the courtyards of Faience.
Here they are heard no more.
Adieu, adieu Provence.

The Gift of Hera

for Dick Davis

In an unbroken line
the heirs of Herakles
harvest their golden trees
and splice the fruitful vine.

Today I play my part.
Paring an apple graft,
I hone an ancient craft
half science and half art.

With an impartial knife
I notch and interlock
host wood and scion stock,
marrying them for life

just as I marry rhymes
and rhythms into lines,
borrowing my designs
from other minds and times.

But where would Virgil be
had Homer not retold
a tale already old
learned at his father's knee?

IV.

Father
of
the
Man

Orchard in Bloom

These seven hundred trees
pillar a pagan church,
a basilica for bees
where seraphic songbirds
promiscuously perch
to blend their melodies
in canticles whose words
the vernal believer
need never decipher.

Nothing Goes to Waste

Rearing on spindly legs
a pair of famished stags
nibble our apple twigs
while does heavy with fawn
file from the woods at dawn
and tiptoe across the lawn
to feast on orchard mast
scattered in harvest haste
before the first hard frost.
Nothing goes to waste.

The Sage Hen

for Katherine V. Murphy

To slake her fledglings' thirst
she dowsed her downy breast
and flew through blowing dust
from the river to her nest.

Now she is distressed,
always dreading the worst
for the flighty brood she nursed
because we do not nest.

The Blighted Tree

for Tessie Buckley Murphy

"Spare that sucker at the root,"
she cautioned as I felled her tree.
Half-blind and eighty-three,
she planned to watch that sprout
blooming and bearing fruit.

Hardy enough to outlast me,
humming with bees and memories,
this offshoot of a blighted tree
spreads its flowery boughs
outside Tessie's shuttered house.

Razing the Woodlot

for Vincent R. Murphy

Here stands the grove our tenant plans to fell.
The homesteaders who planted this tree claim
fled North Dakota when the Dust Bowl came.
Their foursquare farmhouse is a roofless shell;
their tended shelterbelt, a den for fox
and dumpground for machinery and rocks.

The woodlot seeds its pigweed in our loam,
and windstorms topple poplars on the field;
but for a few wasted acres' yield
we'll spare the vixen and her cubs their home
and leave unburied these decaying beams
to teach us the temerity of dreams.

February

A coyote hides in a draw
under a bale of straw,
dreaming of gopher mounds
on dusty lekking grounds
where prairie chickens dance,
newborn pronghorns prance
and killdeers caterwaul.
So hunters dream of fall.

Mother's Day

Mothers gathered from miles around
when the mare foaled on Mother's Day.
One lady's bonnet blew away
and cartwheeled over the trodden ground.
The mare ate it without remorse,
then groomed her newborn's glossy coat.
He whinnied as if to clear his throat:
"Excuse me. I am a little horse."

Feathers

I.

A warbler yellower
and smaller than a flower
    trills
among the daffodils.

II.

Sipping a cordial from
July's geranium
a humming ruby throat
    floats
flaunting its showy coat.

III.

    Fog.
A pheasant hunter slogs
as his quartering dogs
    romp
through a muddy cattail swamp.

IV.

A blizzard-blown bunting
no one would dream of hunting
    spins
in the finger-drifting winds.

Toast

After we sail
the landlocked sea
and bury a rail
in the seething lee,
after we scale
slippery screes
or break a trail
with worn-out skis,
home from the hill
and scraggy swale,
home from the kill
with many a quail,
we hoist a beer
to toast each other.
Cheers to my dear
and only brother!

Felis Horribilis

Vaulting the frozen river
like grouse flushed from cover
startled bucks and does
scatter through the snows.
No cougar crouches
at the forest's fringes,
only a black tomcat
sporting a white cravat.

The Fecund Coming

Flames leap from the logs.
What ruffed beast in the glare
slouches toward my knees?
Pouncing upon my lap,
he purrs at the Yule fire,
turns in a furry gyre
and curls as though to nap
for twenty centuries
while round the rocking chair
reel my indignant dogs.

Diktynna Thea

for José Ortega y Gasset

We hunker by the fire
to read a hunter's praise
of Socrates. The blaze
leaps like a dog's desire
when ducks circle a blind,
then gutters and burns low.
Outside the moonlit snow
flows in a bitter wind.
I scratch my bitch's withers.
She sighs for whirring Huns,
cackling cocks, blasting guns
and a mouthful of feathers.

Passel O' Pups

Bonny bairnies, black an' fine,
wi yir yivver souks an' ruggs,
will ye be guid hountin dugs
worthy o' yir faither's line?
Will ye busk an' tak them doun,
frantik pairtrick, crouchin grouse,
an' the Deil's ain phaisant louse?
Will ye ding the raibbit broon?
Lak the dun deir ye maun lepe
owre yon scraggy, stany hill
whaur the wund blaws lood an' shrill,
sare an' snell, whaur muckle depe
drifts the snaw. Drink yir fill,
glazie beasties; souk an' slepe.

A Dog Young and Old

I. Obedience

I am the Alpha male,
dispenser of her meat.
With drooping ears and tail
she trembles at my feet.
Leader of the pack,
I growl a wolfish note,
tumble her on her back
and bite her furry throat.

II. First Spring

Daily the flocks increase
as the floodwaters rise.
Celebratory cries
of homecoming geese
boggle my puppy's brain.
Out of the melting snows
she lifts her curious nose
to scent the impending rain.

III. Skunked Again

Flurries of hoarfrost fall
like silver maple leaves
as laggard snowgeese call
and my retriever weaves.
Hot on a bird, she speeds
into the frozen fen.
From the last clump of reeds
bursts an indignant hen.

IV. Dog Heaven

Sprawled in the pickup box,
my old bitch is half-dead.
Her slashed teat needs stitches,
her nettled nose twitches,
and nine gutted pheasant cocks
pillow her dreaming head.

The Blind

Gunners a decade dead
wing through my father's mind
as he limps out to the blind
bundled against the wind.

By some ancestral code
fathers and sons don't break,
we each carry a load
of which we cannot speak.

Here we commit our dead
to the unyielding land
where broken windmills creak
and stricken ganders cry.

Father, the dog and I
are learning how to die
with our feet stuck in the muck
and our eyes trained on the sky.

Elegy for Diktynna

Go if you must, and swim
the dim waters of Acheron
        for Actaeon.

When my engraved grouse gun
passes to someone else's son,
        I'll whistle "Come."

Air

Come Diktynna come—
once more the mourning dove
coos in the blooming plum.

Mark the wood duck drake
plummeting through a grove,
and greenheads in the brake.

When fledglings try their wings
and waves of migrants heave
skyward in widening rings,

you will not heed my gun
nor leave this grassy grave—
your hunting days are done.

Drowse Diktynna drowse
lulled by a humming hive
under the apple boughs.

So stealthily stole death
my love could not retrieve
your evanescent breath.

Father of the Man

Last night I sought the lost scout in my dreams.
    After a twilight slog
    I found him in a bog
sobbing amid a maze of braided streams.

Bloodied by leeches, maddened by the buzz
    of deerflies round his ears
    and half-blinded by tears,
the lad had no notion where he was—

yards from a hummock which two pathways crossed.
    His small hand holds me fast
    though thirty years have passed
and I confuse the searcher with the lost.

The Path Mistaken

*"An ye do naught else, lad, plant mony
a tree."*
—last words of The Douglas

In a leafless wood I lose my way.
Too many winding paths have crossed:
more choices to make than Robert Frost—
most of them wrong—and now I stray
with an empty bag on a grouseless day.

Like a winded fox I hesitate
but here is terrain I recognize.
A stand of white pines crowns this rise
and a plaque from Nineteen Sixty Eight.
Tipping my flask, I contemplate

the scouts I led above this lake
slashing through brush and tangled vines
to plant a thousand seedling pines.
My back and shoulders recall the ache
of hard work done for the forest's sake.

For the forest's sake or perhaps to ease
the prospect of a childless life.
At forty I've neither son nor wife,
no plays, novels or symphonies,
but credit me with this tract of trees.

The Track of a Storm

Bastille Day, 1995

We grieve for the twelve trees we lost last night,
pillars of our community, old friends
and confidants dismembered in our sight,
stripped of their crowns by the unruly winds.
There were no baskets to receive their heads,
no women knitting by the guillotines,
only two sleepers rousted from their beds
by fusillades of hailstones on the screens.
Her nest shattered, her battered hatchlings drowned,
a stunned and silent junko watches me
chainsawing limbs from corpses of the downed,
clearing the understory of debris
while supple saplings which survived the blast
lay claim to light and liberty at last.

Haunted by Waters

for Norman Maclean

You strive to roll your prose
as the river in your youth
rolled cobbles round and smooth,
but words are lunker trout
lurking under willows
or lolling in the shallows.

You long to launch your flies
like an artist from the past—
a canvas-vested Marlowe
crafting cutthroat tragedies
with every shadow-cast
at the Blackfoot's braided eddies.

Reckless Marlowe, feckless Paul—
whose fault is a tavern brawl?
With empty creel you hobble
beside a silted channel,
mourning the stricken river
and your murdered brother.

Summer Snow

When stoneflies hatch
on the Yellowstone,
browns and rainbows snatch
every feathery fly flown
from the talused banks.
Fish and give thanks.

Faint Thunder

Once I was a hunter.
Now I am a dove
flitting through the sky.
Unaware, my love
grieves at my grave.
Better he than I.

V.

Early
Poems

Before The Fall

I am no Perseus come to swing a blade.
I bring my own Medusa, unlovely maid
haunting the hedges of my unkempt maze,
laughing at the mirror before she slays.
No Minotaur roars into the fray
while I seduce the waif I must betray.
No ship awaits me, straining at the tide.
I am Ariadne the jilted bride;
I am Adam before the Angels fell,
the rib restored, androgynous as hell.

Ganymede and the Eagle

A sudden blow, and outstretched talons clasp
the struggling boy, pinning him to the rock
from which he piped to his indifferent flock.
Helpless, he wriggles in the raptor's grasp
while his rapacious captor strips its prize,
tearing his flimsy chiton with its beak.
Now bearing him to the Olympic peak,
the eagle screams its triumph to the skies
but does not let its naked victim drop.
Zeus has assumed the likeness of a bird
to save this shepherd from the common herd.
Filling Jove's cup when the Immortals sup,
kissing the Father of the Gods to sleep,
how could he miss the maidens or the sheep?

The Sacrifice

While Xerxes' fleet labored along the coast,
ten of his triremes crossed the open sea
to reconnoiter the Hellenic host
his spies expected at Thermopylae.
Falling upon three Greek ships near the shore,
the Persians boarded their outnumbered foes
to pick a victim for their god of war.
Leo of Troezen was the youth they chose,
handsomest sailor in the Argive ranks.
Stripping the breastplate from his manly chest,
they spilled his entrails on the sea-bleached planks.
And nobody was terribly distressed
that one so handsome died a sacrifice.
The gods bestow their blessings for a price.

For the Theban Dead

The Sacred Band is overthrown.
Lover by slaughtered lover sleeps
while iron-hearted Macedon
sags on his bloody horse and weeps.

340 B.C.

I.

Alexander and his lover
rest their stallions by a brook.
Sprawled on a bank of clover,
the Prince ponders Plato's book:

" *With noble word or deed*
mortal man fathers a scion
fairer than fruit of human seed.
Are we brutes, Hephaistion?

Must we hunt this upland wood
till the chase leaves us lame?
Let our arrows target the Good
and fell the fleet stag of Fame."

II.

Tinkling with rings, the King of Kings
rises late from his perfumed bed.
Soothingly a slavegirl sings.
Eunuchs groom the sovereign head.

Darius loathes his duties royal—
cozening satraps' embassies,
boiling litigants in oil.
Someone must fill his treasuries.

Under the gilded palace roof
His Highness never dreams of shame—
Persia crushed by an upstart youth
and gay Persepolis aflame.

Waiting for Octavian

Alexandria danced and drank as though
Rome came with overtures of love, not war.
While the defeated Antony lay low,
scores of the dishevelled courtiers swore
a giddy pact to perish with their Queen.
Egypt herself was scarcely to be seen,
closeted with her toxins. Which was quick,
which least painful? Slaves condemned to die
swallowed her hellebore or arsenic
and writhed beneath the Queen's appraising eye.
Monkshood, nightshade, hemlock, or aconite,
what could be subtler than the aspic's bite?

The Limits of Empire

Not for Trajan the fabled Khyber Pass,
Parthia, Bactria, the leagues of grass
Alexander's tireless horsemen swept.
Having confirmed the world's enormity,
an old man bested by infirmity
collapsed at the Euphrates' mouth and wept.

The Challenge

What polished flattery or slippery truth
tempted your marble athlete from his plinth?
Now that you've won so statuesque a youth,
what brazen gates safeguard this Hyacinth?
You keep no sentries posted at your doors,
no trusted eunuchs to massage your prize,
nor spies to poison your competitors
who pace the racetrack with appraising eyes.
What powder or potion, what force of arms
mustered at midnight will forestall your boy
from yielding to a younger rival's charms?
What Troy or Parthia can you destroy
to make yourself his hero? And what less
would make you worthy of his loveliness?

To an Arrogant Young Man

Narcissus, gazing in a forest pool,
knelt on the moss to kiss his mirrored face
and drowned in his own image's embrace,
a fate befitting such a haughty fool
whom you rival in cruelty, but who
was twenty times more beautiful than you.

Hadrian Bereaved

The White Nile falls. Osiris dies.
Egypt wails under winter squalls.
In the embalmers' pungent halls
my lover's mummy lies,
marvel of mortuary art
with myrrh and spikenard in its veins.
A gold-enameled cask contains
the ashes of his heart.

I shall not slay my slaves for him.
Rather I'll found a cult of grief,
commissioning bronze and bas-relief
lest Stygian shadows dim
an old man's image of the dead.
Flushed with the sweat of victory,
he'll glisten in my memory
as I crown his tousled head.

Paul Among the Corinthians

City where mighty Eros reigns,
swarming with whores and lovesick boys,
Corinth certainly entertains.
No athlete can exhaust her joys.
Through dearth or feast, siege or peace,
Corinth drains the loins of Greece.

Stalking the square where sophists speak,
bearded, balding, barbaric Paul
slanders love in vagabond Greek.
Herms and Aphrodites quail
as the saint preaches rectitude,
censuring the nude and lewd.

Two genteel youths, bored by the row,
stroll from the plaza arm in arm
to renew their ephebic vow.
Repairing to the elder's farm,
they call for wine and roasted dove
to placate the offended God of love.

The Temple of Attis

mutato nomine

On Cybele's holy hill
the equinoctial throngs
thrilled to the screech of shrill
flutes and clashing gongs

as priests of Attis wrung
sacrificial necks
or pressed the reckless young
to slash away their sex.

Trampling the wine-dark mud,
they hanged an effigy
smeared with fresh bull's blood
on the sacred cedar tree.

Now on that hoary hill
where eunuchs laved their hands
in the blood of boy and bull
the throne of Peter stands.

The Resurrection

Though art and learning currently decline,
centuries hence in some monastic crypt
a thirsty monk may find my manuscript
propping a butt of sacramental wine.
Drying its mildewed pages in the sun,
he'll read my panegyrics to the past
and share them with a fellow pederast.
So was Catullus spared oblivion.

The Confession

Heavens, I haven't finished sinning yet!
Ready no cell, no bed of nails for me;
read me no screeds in praise of chastity.
Let me sink deeper in the Devil's debt.
I must become disgustingly depraved
to magnify God's glory when I'm saved.

From the Courier's Pouch

As You Like It made its debut last night.
A pretty flight of poetry it was,
though I'll forewarn you that the plot was slight.
Now all the Blackfriar's gossips are abuzz;
rumors are even mongered at Gray's Inn—
not about Shakespeare's play, which all adore,
but the boy actor who plays Rosaline.
They whisper tales of his backstage amour
for his confrére cast in Orlando's part,
who spurns his private overtures with scorn
while publicly courting a vulgar tart.
Such ironies were scarcely to be borne—
a boy playing a girl who plays a boy,
feigning to woo the author of his woe
while wretchedly contriving to be coy.
We in the know thought he stole the show.

La Fou Anglaise

Shakespeare misleads us in his parting scene
between Richard and Isabelle, his queen.
She: "Must we be divided, must we part?"
He: "Hand from hand, my love, and heart from heart."
In fact we know the queen was only ten,
which freed the king to play with fey young men
whose like the straitlaced barons hadn't seen
since Gaveston fell victim to their spleen.
Then, having slain the royal favorite,
they sat their sovereign on a red-hot spit;
and one wonders if Edward's dying screams
mightn't have troubled his great-grandson's dreams.

The Philosopher-King

"Why is that gallant
  cavalryman chained?"
Frederick inquired,
  brandishing his cane.
"We found him *in flagrante*
  with his mare, gracious Sire,"
sheepish guards explained.
"Dunderheads!" thundered
  the king indignantly.
"Don't clap him in chains.
  Put him in the infantry!"

The Apotheosis of General Count Deitrich von Hulsen-Haesler

Kaiser Wilhelm and the General Staff
are frolicking in the grand salon.
Fritz Krupp and the All-Highest laugh
at the salacious goings-on.
Young soldiers clad as Grecian swains
bear cups for the besotted guests
while the orchestra's rococo strains
vie with a chorus of Prussian jests.
General Count Deitrich von Hulsen Haesler,
sportive chief of the cabinet,
has driven in haste from Dressler
to attend the Kaiser's bawdy fete.
He prances in wearing a pink tutu
brutally corseted at the waist.
He clumsily pirouettes, turns blue,
and suffers a cardiac arrest.
Panic seizes the grand salon:
will word leak to the English press?
Kaiser and Cronies Carry On;
General Drops Dead in Ballet Dress!
The Kaiser, utterly mortified,
orders his underlings to keep mum
and surreptitiously slips outside.
When the morticians finally come,
the revellers have scattered in dismay.
The general's corpse is no longer warm.
His tutu will have to be cut away
to bury the Count in uniform.

Precepts of Governance

Praise and promote the basest men:
you'll fear no rivalry.
Cheapen the rich and rare for them:
you'll see no thievery.

Never trouble the rabble's minds:
thinking disturbs their sleep.
Fill their bellies, cane their behinds,
and tax them till they weep.

after Lao-Tsu

The Drunken Sage

An old pine is entwined with vines.
Lolling under its twisted trunk,
a monk is gloriously drunk.
He has no taste for vintage wines
prized by the Manchu Emperor.
Contemplating the world's distress
and love's exquisite bitterness,
he sips a cup of vinegar.

Et Tu Brute

Western Tibet, 1200 A.D.

A painted mummer strikes a temple gong
hailing the hero of an epic poem—
the King of Ling, titled "Gesar of Khrom."
Truly, Caesar, the arm of Rome is long.

The Rape of Tibet

The *I Ching* summons me to its shelf.
Over the lines my fingers range.
The superior man resigns himself
to the immutable law of change.

Dreaming of Li Po

Those whom death separates
soon dry their weeping eyes,
but those whom life separates
exhaust their nights in sighs.

I fear the yellow fever
that lurks in the land of Lu,
for since you crossed the river
I've heard no word from you.

Beyond the forest's fastness
your soul slips in my dreams
over the snow-bound passes
and roaring mountain streams.

Ensnared in Heaven's nets,
you cannot stretch your wings.
I wake as the pocked moon sets
and the first warbler sings.

Fathomless are the seas
with waves huge and angry.
Numberless are the trees
and the dragons hungry.

after Tu Fu

The Mustard Seed Garden

Distant, the tumults of a passing age.
Heaven and the Jade Emperor dwell near,
and I could spend a profitable year
lost in the landscape on this yellowed page.
Perched on a verge between two twisted pines
teeters a thatch and bamboo hermitage.
On the veranda stands a Taoist sage
who smiles benignly at the world's confines.
Drowned in the lake, unearthly mountains float
as a stray catspaw heels a fishing skiff.
In a pavilion shadowed by the cliff
a courtesan quavers a mournful note.
Crickets and frogs have hushed to hear her sing.
The sage and I stand spellbound, listening.

Sunset at The Getty

Framed by the villa's fluted colonnades,
the ocean shimmers as the sunlight fades.
Under an arch the frescoed stucco glows;
swallows swoop through the trellised porticos.
In the courtyard a pair of brazen fawns
browse on the topiary and the lawns.
Within are Getty's prized antiquities—
his Lysippos, the Lansdowne Herakles,
red-figured ware, Roman sarcophagi—
gallery after marble gallery.

Shunning the rooms of garish French antiques,
I seek the stelae of the ancient Greeks.
Mournful Orpheus mouths the threnody
which won the freedom of Euridice.
Beside him stand two daughters of the Muse,
half bird, half woman, bane of sailing crews.
Even the Sirens cease their serenade,
outsung by the bard of that dark glade
where Hades hides away his purloined bride
and Gettys of antiquity reside.

A hailstorm of Vesuvian lapilli
buried the first Villa dei Papiri.
Guided by prints its learned looters drew,
Getty built it anew in Malibu,
choosing with geologic irony
this shaky site for his facsimile
where any oilman might foresee The Quake
toppling polished columns in its wake.
When feral pigs pilfer the bedded herbs
and turkeys have their catchments at its curbs,
what Philhellenes will come here to exhume
the treasures of the Getty from their tomb?

Notes

Harvest of Sorrows: "Barrows" are castrated pigs.

Center Pivots: Field-sized circular sprinklers. Canola, also known as rapeseed, blooms yellow and is often grown under irrigation in the High Plains.

Songs of the North: "Brash" is a mass of floating ice fragments. "Felsenmeer" is frost-shattered rock, commonly found on high mountain ridges or at sea level in the Arctic and Antartic.

Je Me Souviens: The motto of Quebec, recalling French defeat on the plains of Abraham outside the old city's walls.

Sinfonietta: "*Da Trowie Burn*" means "the troll stream," where legendary fiddlers evaded music-starved denizens of the underworld. Aly Bain is the fiddler for the Celtic band, Boys of The Lough.

La Langue Des Troubadours: "*Benvengut*" is the Provençal version of the French greeting "*bienvenue.*" "*Que planh e plor*" means "who complain and cry."

Felis Horribilis: *Ursus horribilis* is the scientific name of the grizzly bear.

La Fou Anglaise: Literally "the English madness," a French term for homosexuality.